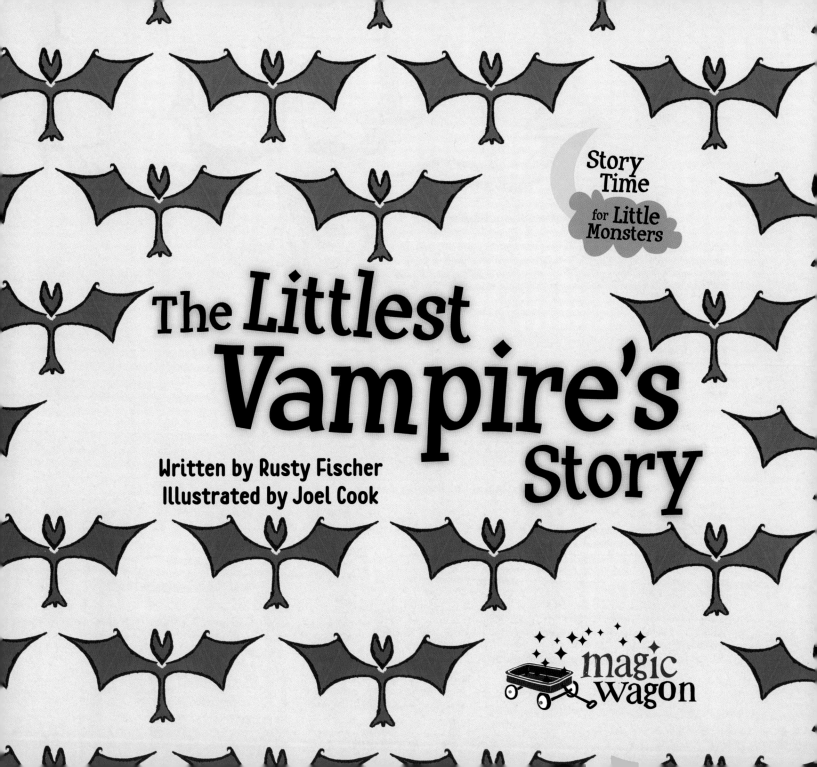

Story Time for Little Monsters

The Littlest Vampire's Story

Written by Rusty Fischer
Illustrated by Joel Cook

magic wagon

visit us at www.abdopublishing.com

Published by Magic Wagon, a division of the ABDO Group, PO Box 398166, Minneapolis, MN 55439. Copyright © 2014 by Abdo Consulting Group, Inc. International copyrights reserved in all countries. All rights reserved. No part of this book may be reproduced in any form without written permission from the publisher.

Looking Glass Library™ is a trademark and logo of Magic Wagon.

Printed in the United States of America, North Mankato, Minnesota.
102013
012014

This book contains at least 10% recycled materials.

Written by Rusty Fischer
Illustrations by Joel Cook
Edited by Stephanie Hedlund and Rochelle Baltzer
Cover and interior design by Renée LaViolette and Candice Keimig

Library of Congress Cataloging-in-Publication Data

Fischer, Rusty, author.
   The littlest vampire's story / written by Rusty Fischer ; illustrated by Joel Cook.
      pages cm. -- (Story time for little monsters)
   Summary: Told in rhyming text, little Vickie the Vampire ignores her mother, and goes out looking for other children to play with--and nearly gets caught outside when the sun comes up.
   ISBN 978-1-62402-020-9
   1. Vampires--Juvenile fiction. 2. Mothers and daughters--Juvenile fiction. 3. Bedtime--Juvenile fiction. 4. Stories in rhyme. [1. Stories in rhyme. 2. Vampires--Fiction. 3. Mothers and daughters--Fiction. 4. Bedtime--Fiction.] I. Cook, Joel, illustrator. II. Title.
   PZ8.3.F62854Li 2014
   813.6--dc23
                                        2013025325

Vickie the Vampire dawdled all night. She would not close her eyes. Her coffin beckoned, dark and cold, but she would *not* get inside!

HUG the SUN

Her mother scowled and scolded her until her fangs were blue. "Now, Vickie, get inside your tomb or the sun will burn through you!"

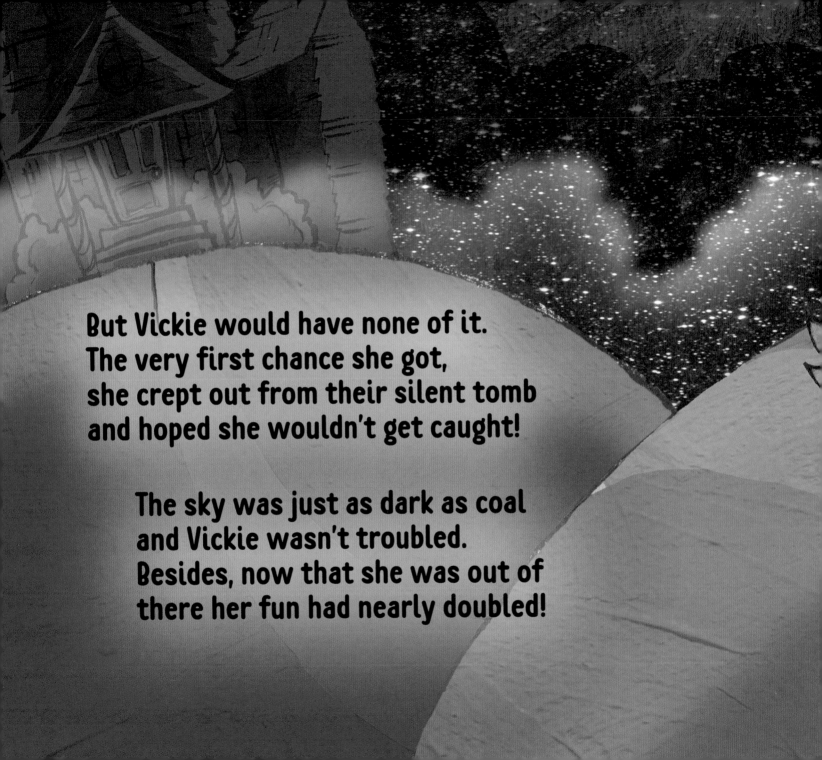

But Vickie would have none of it.
The very first chance she got,
she crept out from their silent tomb
and hoped she wouldn't get caught!

The sky was just as dark as coal
and Vickie wasn't troubled.
Besides, now that she was out of
there her fun had nearly doubled!

She crept right through the cemetery,
skulking through the night.
She hoped to find some little friends
who would not die from fright . . .

. . . just because her teeth were long
and sharpened at the tip.
Why, it took her sixteen weeks
to remember not to bite her lip!

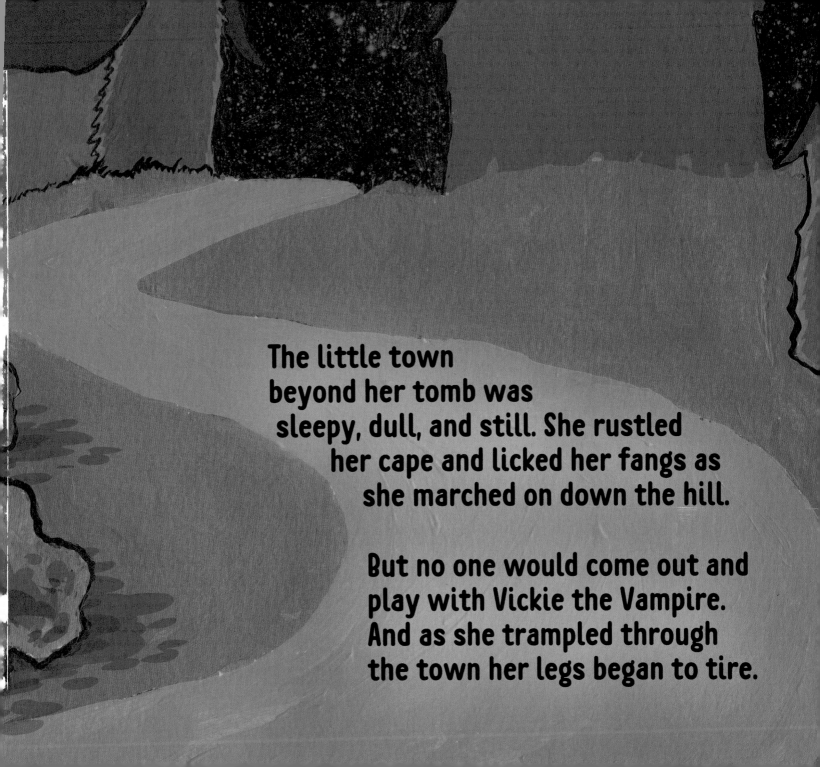

The little town
beyond her tomb was
sleepy, dull, and still. She rustled
her cape and licked her fangs as
she marched on down the hill.

But no one would come out and
play with Vickie the Vampire.
And as she trampled through
the town her legs began to tire.

So she rose into the night
and peeked into high bedrooms.
She was careful not to get mowed
down by witches on their brooms!

The children nestled in
their beds with pinched up
eyes and dreamy smiles.
It went on like that, as
far as Vickie could see, for
miles and miles and miles.

So finally Vickie walked back home, realizing her mother was right. There was no reason to leave the tomb in the middle of the night.

There were no children out at play, no one to call her friend. And so she skulked away from town, her night had come to an end.

Night! Oh no, where
had it gone?
Now the sky
had brightened.
Little Vickie was
far away from
her tomb and
very frightened.

For something
strange had
happened while
Vickie sought a human bud.
Now the sun was on the rise,
turning the horizon the color of blood!

Her mother was right all along,
and now Vickie the Vampire would burn!
"Oh why, oh why," she wondered aloud,
"do I never, ever learn?"

She ran and ran through the town.
The sun chased her all the way home.
She swore if she made it back safely,
from her tomb she would no longer roam.

The sun was looming right at her back. She could feel its rays burning her skin. Vickie knew that even if she could reach her tomb she'd never make it all the way in.

But then as she stumbled, someone held out a hand, the skin both familiar and cold. Her mother was there, with a smile on her face and a coffin 100 years old!

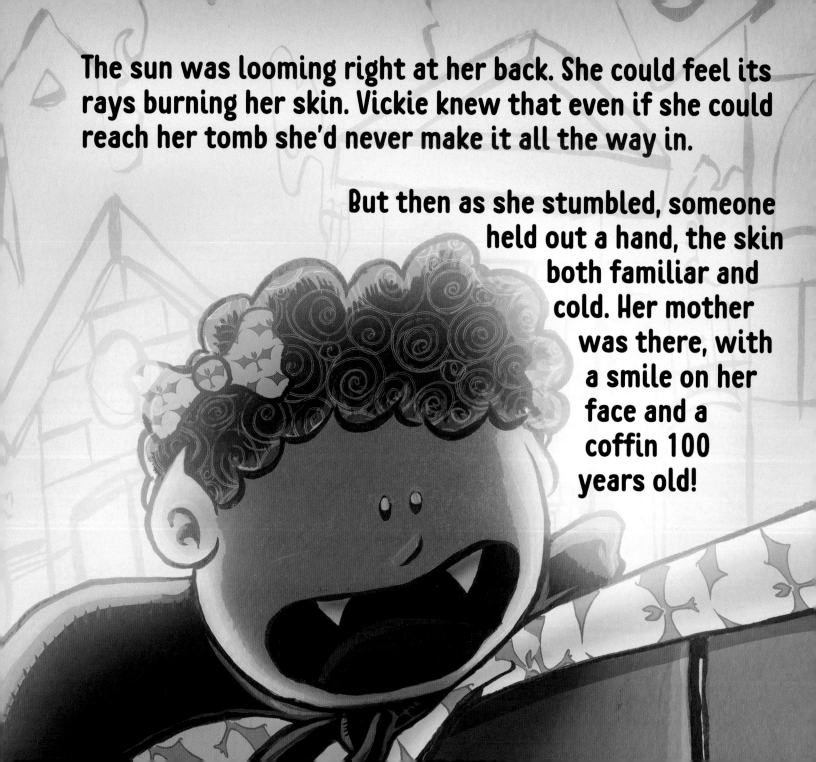

Mother had dragged it from home to meet Vickie before she turned to toast. And if she'd ever been glad to see her mother, Vickie figured right now was the most!

"Get in!" Mother said, as she opened the top. She shoved Vickie the Vampire inside. Then she slammed the door shut, making sure that neither of them fried!

And once they were safe in the coffin and the sun was high in the sky, Vickie's mother smoothed her hair and said, "*Now* will you let me sing you a lullaby?"